100 Grumpy Animals

by

Beast Flaps

GrumpyAnimals.com

For my Son

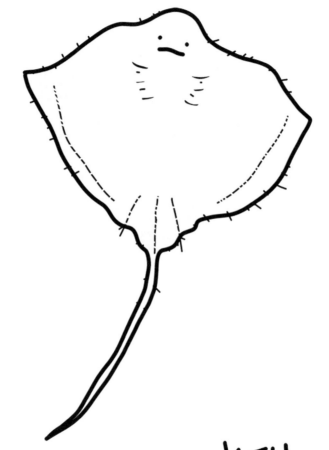

I WILL LOW-KEY
FUCK YOUR SHIT UP

WHO'S BEEN SAYING
I WEAR SHEEP'S
CLOTHING?

I FEEL LIKE I'M JUST BANGING MY HEAD AGAINST THE WALL

AND THERE WAS
DEFINITELY <u>no</u> OTHER
NAME AVAILABLE?

I LITERALLY DON'T
BELONG IN THIS
ENVIRONMENT

GOO GOO
GA FRICKIN JOOB

DO WE ALL NEED
TO BE DOING THIS?

I'M ABOUT
TO LOSE MY SHIT
ANY MINUTE

HAVE A LOVELY
THANKSGIVING
YOU SICK FUCKS

QUIT THROWING
MY FOOD IN THE
TRASH

TOUCAN PLAY
THAT GAME SISTER

BE HONEST, I LOOK
LIKE A TIT DON'T I?

I'm NEVER DOING
THAT AGAIN

AH NUTS

CE jour NE PEUT
PAS EMPiRER

OH Hi, I'm jUST GOnnA SPiT On you REAL Quick

WHATS WRONG WITH
A QUICK SQUEEZE?

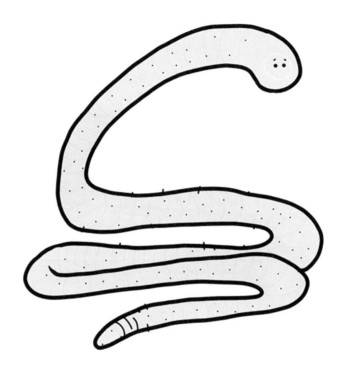

IF YOU'RE HAPPY
AND YOU KNOW IT
CLAP YOUR HANDS

ONCE I GET MY SHIT
TOGETHER IT'S OVER
FOR YOU BITCHES

PRETENDING TO BE ASLEEP IS EASIER THAN DEALING WITH YOUR SHIT

I EAT THINGS
THAT DISAGREE
WITH ME

I DO NOT APPROVE

OK BUT SERIOUSLY
THOUGH WHY DO
I EVEN EXIST

I AM NOT
YOUR HERO

WHAT'S THE MATTER, NEVER SEEN A UNICORN BEFORE?

I HAVE ZERO BUCKS
LEFT TO GIVE

BUT I DIDN'T TELL
THEM ANYTHING

IVE HAD IT
WITH EWE!

TO BE HONEST,
I THOUGHT THERE
WOULD BE MORE
SEX

QUACK
F***ING
QUACK

I'm TRYING my BEST
TO TAKE you SERiOuSLY

PLEASE CALL ME
CUTE ONE MORE
FUCKING TIME

DiD you just
ASSUME my GENDER?

SEE SOMETHING
YOU LIKE, PERVERT?

I FEEL BLUE

I'm just like you
except I'm a
little otter

HOW ABOUT I SHOW
YOU WHAT ELSE I CAN
BURY MY HEAD in

SHIT'S ABOUT
TO BLOW UP YO

I'M A MURDER UNIT

I'm NOT GRUMPY,
I'm JUST RETIRED

QUIT CHECKING ME OUT,
I'm NOT in SEASON

NOT TODAY SORRY,
BUSY SNIFFING BUTTS

DON'T CROSS ME

GUESS I'LL DIE

LESS TALKING AND
MORE BREAD THROWING
PLEASE ASSHOLE

FEELING CUTE, MIGHT EAT SOMETHING ALIVE LATER...

AM I A FUCKING
JOKE TO YOU ?

I DON'T REMEMBER
AGREEING TO THIS

YOU'RE MAKING ME
ALMOST NOT WANT
TO HUG YOU

I'VE GOT THE
HUMP

I KNOW LOTS
OF TRICKS
ACTUALLY

you looking
at my little
hooters?

HONK HONK
MOTHERCLUCKERS!

IT'S OKAY DEAR
I KNOW WE CAN'T
ALL BE THIS FABULOUS

WOULD IT HURT
TO GET A HUG
AROUND HERE?

IF YOU'RE GOING TO
DANGLE THAT HERE
I'M GOING TO CHEW IT

I Ain't your DEER

my LAUGHTER is my
CRY FOR HELP

VERY PLEASED
TO EAT YOU

Hickory Dickory Dock
MOTHERF***ERS

I GIVE UP

YEAH, I'M GONNA NEED
THAT SANDWICH

I'M SURROUNDED
BY STUPIDITY

WHY DO I ALWAYS
HAVE TO GO FIRST?

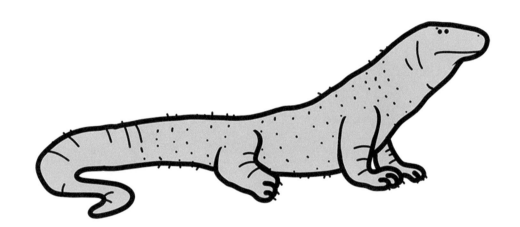

DON'T MAKE ME
BREATHE ON YOU

I'M TIRED OF
YOUR SHIT

MY REAL STRENGTH
IS MAKING YOU
BELIEVE YOU'RE IN
CHARGE

THIS IS STILL
THE BEST DAY
EVER.

OH GROW UP

I AM IN THE
BLOODY ROOM
you KNOW!

I KEEP MY DISTANCE
BECAUSE I'LL JUST END UP
HURTING YOU

I WISH I HAD A
BiG HEAVY SWORD
STRAPPED TO MY FACE
SAID NOBODY EVER

you DONT HAVE A
LEG TO STAND on

I'm NOT GOOD IN
THE MORNINGS BUT
I'm VERY BAD AT NIGHT

I'M A LITTLE SNAPPY
IN THE MORNINGS

ARE WE DOING THIS
KISS OR WHAT? THIS
PRINCE HAS SHIT TO DO

NOW YOU'VE GOT
MY FLAPS
ALL WORKED UP

I JUST CAN'T SEE
IT HAPPENING

WHAT'S FOR LUNCH?
LET ME TAKE A
WILD FUCKING GUESS

SOMEBODY LOOKIN'
FOR AN ASS WHOOPIN'?

BAH

I WILL NEVER LET YOU
GO. UNTIL I HEAR
BONE BREAK

I'M JUST HERE
TO DO THE
BEAR Minimum

I LITERALLY
CAN'T FEEL
MY TESTICLES

ARE YOU JUST
HERE FOR THE
BOOBIES?

ALL THE GUYS THINK

I'M A BOAR

OH BULLOCKS

IT'S "MA'AM"
THANK YOU VERY MUCH

THERE'S A HOLE in
YOUR SOCK SO now
I WILL MURDER YOU

HOW ABOUT I SIT ON YOUR FACE AND WE CAN SEE IF THAT CHANGES COLOR

NO MATTER WHAT
I DO, I NEVER SEEM
TO PROSPER

WELL,
CLUCK IT

SUCK MY
TIDDIES

NEW PHONE,
WHO DIS?

I FEEL LiKE WE'RE
SiDESTEPPiNG
THE iSSUE

WHOOP
DE DOODLE
DOO

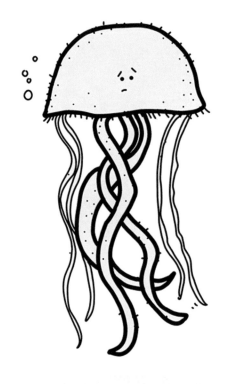

WANT TO HOLD
HANDS OR NAH?

Fin

GrumpyAnimals.com

Made in United States
Troutdale, OR
12/10/2024

26258179R00064